★ SPORTS GREATS ★

TOP 10 SHOOTERS AND SCORERS IN BASKETBALL

David Aretha

Enslow Publishing
101 W. 23rd Street
Suite 240
New York, NY 10011
USA
enslow.com

Published in 2017 by Enslow Publishing, LLC.
101 W. 23rd Street, Suite 240, New York, NY 10011

Library of Congress Cataloging-in-Publication Data

Names: Aretha, David.
Title: Top 10 shooters and scorers in basketball / David Aretha.
Other titles: Top ten shooters and scorers in basketball
Description: New York : Enslow Publishing, 2017. | Series: Sports Greats | Includes bibliographical references and index. | Identifiers: LCCN 2015045459| ISBN 9780766075641 (Library Bound) | ISBN 9780766075610 (Paperback) | ISBN 9780766075627 (6-pack)
Subjects: LCSH: Basketball—Offense—United States—Juvenile literature. | Basketball players—Rating of—United States—Juvenile literature.
Classification: LCC GV889 .A74 2017 | DDC 796.323092/2—dc23
LC record available at http://lccn.loc.gov/2015045459

Printed in the United States of America

To Our Readers: We have done our best to make sure all website addresses in this book were active and appropriate when we went to press. However, the author and the publisher have no control over and assume no liability for the material available on those websites or on any websites they may link to. Any comments or suggestions can be sent by e-mail to customerservice@enslow.com.

Photos Credits: Cover, pp. 1, 44 Ezra Shaw/Getty Images Sport/Getty Images; throughout book, Andrew Rich/E+/Getty Images (basketball texture background); p. 5 Mitchell Leff/Getty Images Sport/Getty Images; pp. 7, 16 George Long/Sports Illustrated/Getty Images; p. 8 James Drake/Sports Illustrated/Getty Images; pp. 11, 12 Focus on Sport/Getty Images; p. 15 Heinz Kluetmeier/Sports Illustrated/Getty Images; p. 19 Carl Skalak/Sports Illustrated/Getty Images; p. 20 Richard Mackson/Sports Illustrated/Getty Images; p. 23 JEFF HAYNES/AFP/Getty Images; p. 24 Manny Millan/Sports Illustrated/Getty Images; p. 27 Otto Greule/Getty Images; p. 28 Al Diaz/Miami Herald/MCT/Getty Images; p. 31 Ronald Martinez/Getty Images Sport/Getty Images; p. 32 Victor Decolongon/Getty Images Sport/Getty Images; pp. 35, 39 Greg Nelson/Sports Illustrated/Getty Images; p. 36 Jason Miller/Getty Images Sport/Getty Images; p. 40 Ron Elkman/Sports Imagery/Getty Images; p. 43 Elsa/Getty Images Sport/Getty Images.

★ Contents ★

★ Introduction ★

Basketball's ten greatest shooters and scorers had very different childhoods. Oscar Robertson lived in a tar-paper shack while Steph Curry was the son of a wealthy NBA player. Kevin Durant and LeBron James grew up poor sons of single moms. Every player in this book overcame obstacles. Michael Jordan didn't make his high school varsity team as a sophomore, which motivated him to get better. Larry Bird quit college and drove a garbage truck before getting serious about his career. Even Curry faced obstacles coming out of high school—no major university was interested in his basketball talents.

All these players were tremendous athletes, but they also had something else in common: an incredible work ethic. They became extraordinary scorers through endless hours of practice. Jerry West played outside on a dirt surface in the winter until his fingers bled. As a young NBA player, Kobe Bryant became obsessed with greatness. During the off-season, he'd drive to a nearby gym and launch two thousand shots a day. Such commitment helped him score 81 points in an NBA game.

The title of this book includes the words "shooters" and "scorers." In basketball, these words have different meanings. A great shooter is extremely accurate from medium range and behind the three-point line. He releases the ball quickly before a defender can get a hand in his face. Jerry West, Ray Allen, and Steph Curry rank among the premier shooters of all time.

A top-notch scorer can find many ways to get the ball in the basket. If open from eighteen feet, he'll swish a jump shot. If guarded tightly, he'll blast around the defender and dribble to the basket for a layup or slam dunk. Great scorers, such as LeBron and Kobe, use a variety of fakes and moves to get an edge on their defenders. Jordan mastered the fadeaway jumper, as described in his chapter.

Note that this book focuses on the game's smaller players—the guards and small forwards. This book's companion Top 10 Towers of Power in Basketball features history's greatest centers and power forwards. Seven-footer Wilt Chamberlain scored 100 points in an NBA game, and center Kareem Abdul-Jabbar scored the most points in NBA history: 38,387.

Though not one of the sweetest shooters in history, LeBron James scores at will in numerous ways, including thunderous slam dunks.

Finally, we salute the phenomenal shooters and scorers who didn't quite make this book. Pete Maravich, George Gervin, Rick Barry, and Reggie Miller could all fill it up from downtown. Hats off, also, to Magic Johnson and John Stockton. Though not huge scorers, those two legendary point guards were tremendous passers, leaders, and winners.

Basketball is a game of many skills, including dribbling, passing, rebounding, and defense. But the main goal is to shoot and score, and these ten men have done it better than anyone else.

★ Elgin Baylor ★

Nickname:	*Mr. Inside*
Teams:	*Minneapolis Lakers, 1958–1960* *Los Angeles Lakers, 1960–1972*
Position:	*Small forward*
Height:	*6'5"*
Year of Note:	***1961–1962, averaging 38.3 points in regular season and 40.6 points in NBA Finals***

Prior to Elgin Baylor, scoring was boring. Players tallied points with layups and outside set shots. Fans rarely leapt from their seats in amazement—until they saw Elgin, The Man of Many Moves.

"Modern basketball began with Elgin Baylor," sportswriter Bob Ryan asserted in an official NBA documentary. "Every single reverse layup, every single between-the-legs dribble, every single spinning move that you see in a routine manner in an NBA game owes its existence to the mind of [Baylor]."

Incredibly, Baylor didn't play basketball as a kid. During his childhood in Washington, DC, in the 1930s and '40s, public playgrounds were off-limits to African Americans. He later emerged at Spingarn High School, where he became the first black player to earn All-Metropolitan honors for Washington. In

1958, he propelled little-known Seattle University to the NCAA championship game.

The Minneapolis Lakers selected the dazzling forward with the first pick in the 1958 NBA Draft. During his first two NBA seasons, Baylor averaged 24.9 and 29.6 points per game (PPG). In 1960, the Lakers moved to Los Angeles, where Baylor took his game to a higher level. With Hollywood celebrities cheering him on in the stands, Elgin averaged 34.8, 38.3, and 34.0 PPG during his first three seasons with the Lakers. On November 15, 1960, he scored 71 points, breaking the NBA record of 64 points, which he had set.

In Game 5 of the 1962 NBA Finals, Boston Celtics legend Bob Cousy watched in amazement as Baylor poured in 61 points. "Elgin was that spectacular," Cousy said in the NBA documentary. "He literally became the first guy who couldn't be stopped."

Tommy Hawkins, who teamed with Baylor on the Los Angeles Lakers, agreed. "He had the greatest variety of shots of anyone," Hawkins told the San

Baylor could hang in the air and shoot from various angles. Overwhelmed defenders, such as this player for the San Francisco Warriors, often wound up fouling him.

Despite legends Elgin Baylor, Jerry West, and Wilt Chamberlain, the Lakers once against lost in the NBA Finals—this time in 1970 to Dave DeBusschere *(left)* and the New York Knicks.

Francisco Examiner. "He would take it in and hang and shoot from all these angles. Put spin on the ball. Elgin had incredible strength. He could post up Bill Russell. He could pass like Magic [Johnson] and dribble with the best guards in the league."

He also could rebound. Though certainly not a giant at six-foot-five, Baylor ranked among the top five in rebounding in each of his first four NBA seasons. In 1960–61, he averaged 19.8 boards per game.

A happy-go-lucky guy, Baylor loved to talk and made a lot of friends around the league. They rooted for him to win an NBA championship, but it never happened. Baylor and shooting legend Jerry West led the Lakers to the NBA Finals seven times, but they always lost. Six times they fell to the Celtics, who had a dominant center in Bill Russell.

Elgin lost much of his athleticism after undergoing major knee surgery in 1965. Yet he helped carry the Lakers to the Finals again in '66, and he didn't retire until October 31, 1971. Ironically, that was the season LA won its first NBA title.

Baylor finished with a career scoring average of 27.4 PPG. To this day, only two NBA players have eclipsed that extraordinary mark: Michael Jordan and Wilt Chamberlain.

★ Oscar Robertson ★

Nickname:	*The Big O*
Teams:	*Cincinnati Royals, 1960–1970* *Milwaukee Bucks, 1970–1974*
Position:	*Point guard*
Height:	*6'5"*
Year of Note:	*1961–1962, averaging 30.8 points, 11.4 assists, and 12.5 rebounds per game*

As a kid in the 1940s, Oscar Robertson didn't dream of playing in the NBA. Heck, the league didn't even exist back then, and he didn't touch a basketball until 1951, when he was in eighth grade. At that time, life's odds were stacked against him. Oscar's impoverished family lived in a tar-paper shack in Indianapolis, Indiana, and he was too short to excel in basketball. But then, during the summer of 1952, something amazing happened.

"I stood 5 foot 8 inches tall then," he wrote in his autobiography, The Big O. "That summer I went to visit my grandparents in Tennessee. When I came back, I was 6 foot 4."

At Crispus Attucks High School, Oscar developed into an unstoppable force. He led his team to forty-five straight victories and two Indiana state championships. He enrolled at the University of Cincinnati, where he took college basketball by

The Big O routinely drove to the basket, but his opponents didn't know if he would continue for a layup, pull up for a jumper, or pass to an open teammate.

storm. Powerfully built at six-foot-five, Robertson swished fadeaway jumpers and scored inside with either hand. The Big O led the nation in scoring as a sophomore (35.1 PPG), junior (32.6 PPG), and senior (33.7 PPG). Each season he was named National Player of the Year.

In 1960, Robertson led the United States to an Olympic gold medal and went number one overall in the NBA Draft. As a rookie with the Cincinnati Royals, he dominated in all phases of the game. In 1960–61, he averaged 30.5 points, 10.1 rebounds, and 9.7 assists per game. He was so exciting that a local rock 'n' roll band created a song and dance called "The Big O." "Dribble to your left, dribble to your right . . . ."

Oscar normally beamed a huge smile but not on the court. "Every game, you had this anger out there," Boston Celtics forward Satch Sanders recalled. "And frown. You would see that frown."

Robertson averaged 25.7 points per game during his NBA career, which ranked tenth in history entering the 2015–16 season.

Robertson beat defenders in so many ways. While in midair, he'd decide whether to shoot or unleash a dazzling pass. After tricking his man with a head fake or pump fake, Robertson would drive past him for a score. He also used his strength and dribbling skills to his advantage. New York Knicks guard Dick Barnett moaned: "If you give him a twelve-foot shot, he'll work on you until he's got a ten-foot shot. Give him six, he wants four. Give him two feet and you know what he wants? That's right, man, a layup."

Throughout basketball history, a triple-double has been a rare, celebrated accomplishment. In 1961–62, Robertson averaged a triple-double: 30.8 points, 12.5 rebounds, and 11.4 assists per game. His 181 career triple-doubles are by far an NBA record.

Robertson played ten seasons with the Royals and four with the Milwaukee Bucks, leading them to the NBA championship in 1971. He topped 30 PPG in six seasons and won the NBA MVP Award in 1963–64. He drew so many fouls while driving to the basket that he ranks fourth all-time in free throws made. Twice he led in free-throw percentage. At the time of his retirement, he ranked second in NBA history in points (26,710) and first in assists (9,887).

In 1974, Oscar hung up his sneakers for good. "I've done the best I could," he said upon retirement. "I've accomplished everything I could have hoped for. It was fun while it lasted."

His opponents were glad he was gone.

★ Jerry West ★

Nickname: *Mr. Clutch*
Teams: *Los Angeles Lakers, 1960–1974*
Position: *Shooting guard*
Height: *6'2"*
Year of Note: *1969–1970, leading the NBA in scoring with 31.2 PPG*

Practice, practice, practice. That's how you get yourself on the NBA logo.

Well, that's how it played out for Jerry West. The official NBA logo—a white silhouette of a left-handed player on a blue and red background—was based on this basketball legend. West rose to glory by dribbling on dirt and shooting against a shed over and over and over.

Born in 1938, Jerry grew up poor and shy in Cheylan, West Virginia. His father worked as a coal-mine electrician and didn't have much time for his six children. Jerry was so frail that he was kept out of organized sports so he wouldn't get hurt. His closest brother, David, died in the Korean War when Jerry was twelve. Jerry's only outlet? Basketball.

For hours at a time, Jerry fired shots at a hoop that was nailed to his neighbor's storage shed. The ground below was dirt—sometimes mud, sometimes snow and ice—but Jerry kept on playing. He dribbled and shot until his fingers bled.

West became so good that he led East Bank High School to the 1956 state championship. He dreamed of leading the University of West Virginia to glory, and in 1959, he took the Mountaineers to the national title game. West cocaptained the 1960 US Olympic team to a gold medal, and then he turned pro. Even in the NBA, he was the best shooter on the floor.

At first glance, West looked like he shot the ball with two hands. Really, his right hand did all the work.

West played his entire fourteen-year career with the Los Angeles Lakers. While high-scoring teammate Elgin Baylor was Mr. Inside, West was Mr. Outside. Jerry released his shot quickly, and he had tremendous accuracy from a long range. The NBA didn't have a three-point line back then, but Jerry bombed away from beyond that distance. "I'm surprised when the ball doesn't go into the hoop," he said. "I think I should make every shot."

Despite his slender frame—six-foot-two, 175 pounds—West also drove hard to the basket. Often teams could stop his drives

West hated to lose, yet he suffered one heartbreak after another in the NBA Finals. His Lakers lost eight times in the Finals, including six times to the Boston Celtics.

only by fouling him. In 1965–66, he led the league with 977 free-throw attempts. The following year, he nailed 88 percent of his free throws.

In 1974, West became the third NBA player to reach 25,000 points. His career average of 27.0 PPG ranks sixth in league history. Four times he averaged more than 30 PPG in a season, and in 1969–70 he led the NBA with 31.2 points per contest.

West excelled in all phases of the game. He led the NBA in assists per game (9.7) in 1971–72, and he leapt so high that he averaged 7.9 rebounds per game in 1961–62. Four times he was named to the NBA All-Defensive First Team. Incredibly, he made the NBA All-Star Game every year of his career.

West focused not on individual achievements but on team success. "He took a loss harder than any player I've ever known," Lakers broadcaster Chick Hearn told National Sports Daily. "He would sit by himself and stare into space. A loss just ripped his guts out."

West led the Lakers to the NBA Finals nine times and won once in 1972. He later coached the Lakers for three seasons and then became their general manager. Even as an executive, he kept on scoring. With West in the front office, the Lakers won seven NBA titles.

★ Larry Bird ★

Nickname:	*Larry Legend*
Team:	*Boston Celtics, 1979–1992*
Position:	*Small forward*
Height:	*6'9"*
Year of Note:	*1985–1986, winning his third NBA MVP Award and third NBA championship*

No one could handle the heat and humidity, nor could the arena. During Game 5 of the 1984 NBA Finals, the temperature in Boston soared to 97 degrees. The old Boston Garden arena felt like a "steam bath," said Los Angeles Lakers coach Pat Riley. A referee became dehydrated, and players struggled for their next breath. But one guy kept flying up and down the court like a bird—Larry Bird.

Boston's superstar forward nailed 15 of 20 shots for 34 points and added 17 rebounds. "Everybody complained about the heat, but I felt great out there," Bird said of the Celtics' victory. "I remember running by the Laker bench and seeing them sitting there sucking in oxygen, and I felt like I could run forever."

Bird earned the nickname Larry Legend because of that game and other extraordinary feats. Though not a great athlete overall, the six-foot-nine forward possessed phenomenal basketball skills.

He out-shot, out-passed, and out-thought opponents on a nightly basis. As a result, he won three NBA MVP Awards in the 1980s and led Boston to three NBA championships. "Larry Bird is so good," Lakers great Magic Johnson said on ESPN, "it's frightening."

Incredibly, Bird once gave up basketball to become a garbage man. While growing up in the small town of French Lick, Indiana, Larry played basketball constantly. "When I was young, I never wanted to leave the court until I got things exactly correct," he said. Bird earned a basketball scholarship to play at Indiana University. But a month into his freshman year, he got homesick and quit school. He then drove a garbage truck and did maintenance work in French Lick. After his father

Bird could see plays developing and respond immediately. He might fire a no-look pass, slither to the rim for a score, or bury a long-range jump shot.

Bird's battles with Magic Johnson *(right)* became legendary. Bird's Celtics won three NBA titles in the 1980s, while Johnson's Lakers prevailed five times in the decade.

died, Larry decided to go back to college. He chose Indiana State University in his hometown.

Bird averaged 30.3 PPG in his three years at Indiana State. "I wasn't real quick, and I wasn't real strong," he said. "So I beat them with my mind and my fundamentals." If Larry sensed his defender was about to lean left, he charged immediately to his right. He could score from a long range or with twisty shots near the basket. Sometimes he shot with his left hand. He passed balls to teammates he couldn't see; he just sensed they were there.

In 1979, experts considered Larry and Michigan State's Magic Johnson two of the greatest college players ever. When they met in that spring's NCAA championship game, twenty million TV viewers tuned in. Michigan State prevailed 75–64. Bird and Magic then dominated the NBA throughout the 1980s.

On March 12, 1985, Larry burned the Atlanta Hawks for 60 points. In one stretch, he swished 32 points in 14 minutes. "When I'm shooting like that," he said, "no one can stop me."

Bird was named First Team All-NBA nine times. He averaged 24.3 PPG for his career while totaling 59 triple-doubles—the most ever by a forward. In 1986–87, he became the first NBA player in history to shoot above 50 percent from the floor, 40 percent from three-point territory, and 90 percent from the free-throw line. The next season, he did it again.

Fellow legend Jerry West said that Larry Bird "is as nearly perfect as you can get in almost every phase of basketball." And that's what made him so frightening.

★ Michael Jordan ★

Nickname:	*Air*
Teams:	*Chicago Bulls, 1984–1993 and 1995–1998* *Washington Wizards, 2001–2003*
Position:	*Shooting guard*
Height:	*6'6"*
Year of Note:	*1995–1996, topping the NBA in scoring (30.4 PPG), winning the NBA MVP Award, leading Chicago to an NBA-record 72 regular-season wins and the NBA title*

In the middle of the night, Michael Jordan awoke in his Utah hotel room. He was sweating and shaking, and his head was spinning. He felt like he was going to die. "I was scared; I didn't know what was happening to me," Jordan said, as told by ESPN.com. "I felt partially paralyzed."

Doctors diagnosed Michael with the flu. No way, they said, would he play in the next contest—Game 5 of the NBA Finals between his Chicago Bulls and the Utah Jazz. MJ spent more than a day in bed. Then, at 3 p.m. on June 11, 1997, he dragged himself out of his hotel room. He headed to the Delta Center for Game 5. Michael looked terrible and felt weak and nauseated. Yet somehow, some way, he played 44 minutes and scored 38 points. His three-pointer with 26 seconds remaining broke an 85–85 tie, and the Bulls prevailed. Afterward, he collapsed into teammate Scottie Pippen's arms.

"This was a heroic effort," Bulls coach Phil Jackson said after the game, "one to add to the collection of efforts that make up his legend."

Jordan led the Bulls to three straight NBA championships, retired to play baseball, then came back to win three more titles in a row. Here he hoists the 1997 championship trophy.

Michael Jordan grew up in Wilmington, North Carolina, where he was a good—but not great—basketball player. As a sophomore at Laney High School, he didn't make the varsity team. "It was embarrassing not making that team," he said, as quoted on ESPN.com. Michael, determined to improve his game, developed into one of the top high school players in the nation. His legend began in the 1982 NCAA championship game, when he hit the winning shot.

In 1984, a month into his rookie NBA season, Michael appeared on the cover of Sports Illustrated next to the headline "A Star Is Born." Jordan averaged 28.2 PPG that season and dazzled fans with his leaping ability. Millions of kids wanted to Be Like Mike. In fact, Nike would go on to sell billions of dollars' worth of his Air Jordan sneakers.

Michael's North Carolina license plate read "M AIR J." Underneath those letters were the state's—and Michael's—motto, "First in Flight."

Michael scored on soaring drives to the basket and thousands of outside shots. He perfected the fadeaway jumper. He would back up against an opponent, turn around, and—while floating backward—shoot the jump shot.

Jordan led the NBA in scoring in ten of his fifteen seasons, including 37.1 PPG in 1986–87. His career average of 30.1 PPG is the all-time record. On March 28, 1990, he burned Cleveland for 69 points. Beyond scoring, MJ was a terrific passer and ball handler, and he was the 1987–88 NBA Defensive Player of the Year. His 2,514 steals rank third all-time. Five times he won the NBA MVP Award.

"Talent wins games," Jordan said, "but teamwork and intelligence wins championships." So did his burning desire to win. Michael, along with masterful coach Phil Jackson and teammate Scottie Pippen, led the Bulls to six NBA titles. They prevailed in 1991, '92, and '93. After Jordan took more than a year off to play professional baseball, Chicago prevailed in '96, '97, and '98. In each NBA Finals that MJ played, he earned the MVP Award.

Michael was the first basketball star to become internationally famous, and historians widely regard him as the greatest player in NBA history. In fact, ESPN rated him the Number One North American Athlete of the Twentieth Century—one spot higher than Babe Ruth.

★ Ray Allen ★

Nickname:	*Sugar Ray*
Teams:	*Milwaukee Bucks, 1996–2003; Seattle SuperSonics, 2003–2007; Boston Celtics, 2007–2012; Miami Heat, 2012–2014*
Position:	*Shooting guard*
Height:	*6'5"*
Year of Note:	*2005–2006, averaging 25.1 PPG and setting an NBA record with 269 three-pointers*

For Ray Allen, 1993–94 would be the biggest season of his life. He was a senior at Hillcrest High School in South Carolina and dead serious about becoming a basketball star. A sweet shooter with a beautiful all-around game, Ray had studied hard in the classroom, too. He was determined to go to a major university and eventually make it to the NBA.

On the opening tip-off of the first game that season, the ball landed in Ray's hands. He romped down the floor, soared to the heavens, and threw down a rim-rattling slam dunk.

In his own basket. Oops!

Fortunately for Ray, his career took off from there. He led Hillcrest to the state championship, earned First Team All-American honors at the University of Connecticut, and became a ten-time NBA All-Star. Allen was a graceful player, smooth and fluid. Mostly he was known for his sugar-sweet shooting. In fact, Ray sank an NBA record 2,937 three-point baskets.

"Ray is hands-down the best shooter in NBA history," said Boston Celtics teammate Nate Robinson. "It's kind of cool just watching him."

Ray was more than just a brilliant basketball player. "He's one of the best people I've ever been involved with," said Connecticut coach Jim Calhoun. Players considered him professional, intelligent, and a great team leader. "He's strikingly handsome," added sportswriter Jon Wertheim, "and he has a million-dollar smile.... [He] speaks in the soothing voice of a pilot pointing out sites of interest below."

Ray grew up all over the world. His father served in the Air Force, and every three years or so his family moved to another military

Allen was such a smooth athlete and sweet shooter that he reminded many fans of Michael Jordan. Though he didn't score as many points as MJ, he certainly was better from the long range.

In both his seasons with Miami, Allen helped the Heat to the NBA Finals. They defeated San Antonio in 2013 but lost the rematch with the Spurs the following year.

base. A natural athlete as a kid, Ray excelled in football, baseball, soccer, and especially basketball. His mother, Flo, encouraged Ray to work hard at basketball and school. He enjoyed both.

"I've always been a reader," Allen told the Boston Globe. "Once I got to the NBA, I picked it up again because I had so many lonely nights where I was on a plane.... So I started reading books more then, started reading things, going to different places in my mind."

Allen played eighteen seasons in the NBA. He twice averaged more than 22 points per game with Milwaukee. In 2005–06, playing for Seattle, he set an NBA record with 269 three-pointers.

Ray scored in various ways. He would dribble hard to the basket, stop suddenly, and then swish a fadeaway jump shot. He would also catch a pass and shoot a medium-range jumper before his defender could react. His 89.4 shooting percentage at the free-throw line ranks among the best in league history. He not only launched a ton of three-point bombs, he also made 40 percent of them—an outstanding rate.

How did Ray perfect his shooting stroke? "It comes down to consistency," he said. "If you want to be a great shooter, you have to shoot the same way every time."

In later years, Allen played for two contending teams, Boston and Miami. He was a supporting player for both and provided wisdom to teammates while hitting big shots at important moments. "Every time he gets the ball, we think it's going in," said Robinson. With Ray on their side, both the Celtics and Heat won NBA championships.

★ Kobe Bryant ★

Nickname: *Mamba*
Team: *Los Angeles Lakers, 1996–present*
Position: *Shooting guard*
Height: *6'6"*
Year of Note: *2005–2006, leading the NBA with 35.4 PPG—the most by any player since 1986–1987*

One day, Kobe Bryant decided to give himself a nickname. He called himself Mamba after a versatile and deadly snake. "The Mamba can strike with 99 percent accuracy at maximum speed, in rapid succession," Bryant said. "That's the kind of basketball precision I want to have." The Mamba can also raise itself four feet off the ground, and it's almost impossible to kill. It's kind of like how Kobe was on January 23, 2006.

He was angry that night—mad at himself and his team. At halftime, his Los Angeles Lakers trailed the Toronto Raptors 63–49. For Kobe, it was time to strike. By driving to the basket and swishing outside shots, he scored 27 points in the third quarter and 28 in the fourth. "He just kept attacking, attacking, attacking—every time he got the ball," teammate Devean George said afterward. The Lakers won 122–104, and Bryant finished with 81

"He's become a giver [or a helpful teammate] rather than just a guy that's a demanding leader."

The son of NBA player Jellybean Joe Bryant, Kobe inherited his dad's talent and passion for the game. By age three, he was already proclaiming he would be an NBA star. At Lower Marion High School in Pennsylvania, Kobe broke Chamberlain's state record for career points. He was a national sensation. For his prom date in 1996, he took Brandy—a superstar singer.

The Lakers drafted Bryant out of high school that June, and in 1997–98, he became the first teenager to play in the NBA All-Star Game. Kobe routinely beat defenders with his quickness and eye-popping moves. Bryant could do anything on the court. He once passed the ball off the backboard to himself and then dunked it. Another time, he nailed a three-pointer with his left hand. His work ethic was off the charts. One summer, he made 100,000 shots!

In 2006–07, Kobe won his second scoring title (31.6 PPG). A year later, he captured the NBA MVP Award. Entering 2015–16, he owned a career scoring average of 25.4—the tenth highest of all time. That year, he became the fourth man ever to play in twenty NBA seasons.

Though injuries had wracked his body, Kobe Bryant was still a giver, still a scorer, and still ready to strike with 99 percent accuracy at maximum speed. He was still Mamba.

★ LeBron James ★

Nickname:	*King James*
Teams:	*Cleveland Cavaliers, 2003–2010 and 2014–present; Miami Heat, 2010–2014*
Position:	*Small forward*
Height:	*6'8"*
Year of Note:	*2012–2013, averaging 26.8 points, 8.0 rebounds, and 7.3 assists per game, and winning the NBA MVP Award and NBA title*

Before each Cleveland Cavaliers home game, LeBron James goes to the scorer's table. He pours powder onto his hands and tosses it high into the air with both arms raised. The crowd jumps to their feet and roars with excitement. They sense that the world's greatest player is about to make magic happen.

Perhaps he'll score 61 points in the game like he did on March 3, 2014. Or maybe he'll record a triple-double, which he has done more than any player of his generation. Or perhaps this powerful six-foot-eight athlete will carry his team to the NBA Finals, which he has done six times. King James led the NBA in scoring in 2007–08 (30.0 PPG) and then won four of the next five NBA MVP Awards.

Many in sports consider LeBron the greatest athlete in the world. "Right now, he's the best," Major League Baseball player Dexter Fowler told ESPN.com in 2015. "He's the most dominant player in the game right now. The guy can do everything. He could play football. I'm sure he could probably play baseball."

Ironically, James's basketball story began on the worst day of his life. On Christmas morning in 1987, three-year-old LeBron received a plastic basketball hoop. His mother, Gloria James, had yet to tell him that her mother, Freda, had died of a heart attack hours earlier. They all lived in Freda's house in Akron, Ohio, and after her mother's death, Gloria couldn't afford to live there.

From ages five to eight, LeBron moved twelve times with his mom. They lived in crime-ridden areas of Akron with gunshots heard in the distance. Scariest of all, LeBron "would sometimes go a few nights without seeing" his mother, he wrote in LeBron's

LeBron beams a smile after winning his second NBA championship with Miami in 2013. For most of his career, he has struggled to deliver a title to Cleveland.

With fellow Cavaliers out with injuries, LeBron became a one-man wrecking crew in the 2015 NBA Playoffs. He averaged 30.1 points, 11.3 rebounds, and 8.5 assists in 20 games.

Dream Team. "I became afraid that one day I would wake up, and she would be gone forever."

When LeBron was in fifth grade, he moved in with an African American family named the Walkers. He finally had a stable life, and he thrived in both school and sports. Eventually, he moved back in with his mother. LeBron excelled so much in basketball that he became the first two-time National High School Player of the Year. Cleveland selected him right out of high school, and he averaged 20.9 PPG as a rookie in 2003–04.

James has made the NBA All-Star team every year since. He shines as a shooter, passer, rebounder, and defender, and he helps make his teammates better. In 2011, he worked on his post-up game with legendary center Hakeem Olajuwon. From there on, James became a dominant scorer around the basket. "His improvement in that area alone transformed our offense to a championship level in 2012," Miami coach Erik Spoelstra told Grantland.com.

One thing LeBron has yet to do as of 2015 is lead the Cavaliers to the NBA championship. In 2010, he became a free agent and chose to sign with Miami, which left Cleveland fans heartbroken. He won two NBA titles with the Heat, and in 2014, he became a free agent again. "I'm coming home," he wrote in Sports Illustrated.

Cleveland fans welcomed LeBron with open arms, and in his first year back he led the Cavaliers to the NBA Finals. They lost to Golden State, but LeBron offered hope for the following season. "I'm not happy with the way things turned out," he tweeted. "I PROMISE to get better."

Clevelanders couldn't wait for another year of magic.

★ KEVIN DURANT ★

Nicknames: KD
Teams: Seattle SuperSonics, 2007–2008; Oklahoma City Thunder, 2008–present
Position: Small forward
Height: 6'9"
Year of Note: 2013–2014, leading the NBA in scoring (32.0 PPG) and winning the NBA MVP Award

Kevin Durant, standing tall in a blue suit, was wiping tears from his eyes. He had just received his 2013–14 NBA MVP Award and was delivering an emotional acceptance speech. He talked about the person who had helped him become the best basketball player in the world: his mom.

In Maryland, Wanda Pratt raised Kevin and his three siblings as a single mother. Times were tough. Wanda worked long hours but still found time to support and inspire her children. "You wake me up in the middle of the night in the summertime, making me run up the hill, making me do push-ups," Durant said during his speech. "You made us believe. You kept us off the street, put clothes on our backs, food on the table. When you didn't eat, you made sure we ate. You went to sleep hungry. You sacrificed for us. You're the real MVP."

Kevin Durant is a gifted young man. He has the height of a power forward, yet he boasts the quickness and athleticism of an NBA guard. Opposing small forwards can't find a way to defend his shots. With his six-foot-nine frame and endlessly long arms, he shoots right over them. And with his laser-like accuracy, the result is frequently two points—or three. If guarded by a bigger man, Kevin will zoom past him, drive to the basket, and finish with a thunderous dunk. He is also a terrific passer, rebounder, and defender.

Durant shares the 2014 NBA MVP Award with the Oklahoma City fans. "We disappoint you sometimes," he said in an earlier speech, "but we try our best every single night to win for you guys."

Despite Durant's enormous talent, rising to the top was a struggle. "I failed so many times," he said during his acceptance speech, "and got back up." Family, coaches, teachers, friends, teammates—they all helped Kevin along the way. It's something he recognizes and appreciates. "I had so much help," he said in his speech. "So many people believed in me when I didn't believe in myself."

Durant is so tall from feet to fingers that he has no trouble shooting over the forwards who try to stop him.

When Durant began his senior season at Montrose Christian School, he was five inches taller than the season before. He dominated and earned All-American honors. The next year, he averaged 25.8 PPG at the University of Texas. He became the first freshman to win the Naismith College Player of the Year Award.

In 2007, the Seattle SuperSonics selected Durant second overall in the NBA Draft. A year later, the team moved to Oklahoma City, where KD put the roar into the Thunder. He led the NBA in scoring four times: 2009–10 (30.1), 2010–11 (27.7), 2011–12 (28.0), and 2013–14 (32.0). In 2012, he led Oklahoma City to the NBA Finals.

"I don't think in the years that I've coached and played . . . there's ever been a more difficult guy to prepare for," said Boston Celtics head coach Doc Rivers. "You really feel like you're wasting your time doing it. He's going to probably score anyway."

Yes, he will. Through 2014–15, Durant ranked fifth in NBA history with 27.3 PPG. In 2012–13, he became the sixth player in the 50-40-90 club. That means he shot more than 50 percent from the floor, 40 percent from three-point land, and 90 percent at the free-throw line. In 2012, he set the US record for most points in a single Olympics: 156.

Wanda Pratt has witnessed all her son's extraordinary achievements. But Durant's mom insists, "I'm most proud of how humble he is."

★ STEPHEN CURRY ★

Nickname:	*Steph*
Teams:	*Golden State Warriors, 2009–present*
Position:	*Shooting guard*
Height:	*6'3"*
Year of Note:	*2014–2015, swishing a league-record 286 three-pointers, winning the NBA MVP Award, and leading the Warriors to an NBA title*

Stephen Curry grew up in the NBA. His father, Dell Curry, rained three-pointers for five NBA teams from 1986 to 2002. As a tot, Steph attended many of his dad's games and practices. In Charlotte, North Carolina, little Curry would fire shots on one half of the court while the Hornets practiced on the other side. At age eleven, he frequently competed in a shooting contest called H-O-R-S-E with Milwaukee Bucks players. "It'd be me, Steph and [Bucks teammate] Vinny Del Negro, and we'd kill everybody," Dell told ESPN.com.

In Toronto, Dell, Stephen, and his younger brother, Seth, often put on a shooting show before Raptors games. Fans went wild as Steph, a junior high student, buried three after three. This was no novelty act. Someday, both Curry boys would—like their father—star in the NBA. Stephen, in fact, would become the most dangerous three-point shooter the game has ever known.

Despite his NBA roots, Stephen struggled to earn respect as a young player. Sure he could shoot—and dribble and pass—but as a high school freshman he stood only five-foot-four. Curry grew to six feet as a senior and earned All-State honors in North Carolina. He wanted to go to Virginia Tech, his dad's alma mater, but they didn't want him—he wasn't good enough, they thought. Only three colleges offered him scholarships: Davidson, Virginia Commonwealth, and Winthrop. None were known for their

Dell Curry *(left)* high-fives his son Stephen during a 2015 NBA All-Star Weekend event. Both rank among the greatest shooters in league history.

Curry not only made an NBA record 286 three-pointers in 2014–15, he also shot them at a sensational rate of 44.3 percent. His release is so quick that opponents struggle to defend him.

basketball prowess, but Davidson would be—because of Stephen.

In 2006–07, Curry set the NCAA record for three-pointers by a freshman with 122. The next year, he canned an NCAA record 162 triples and dazzled the nation in the NCAA Tournament. Steph led tiny Davidson College—with only 1,800 students—to stunning tourney upsets over Gonzaga, Georgetown, and Wisconsin by scoring 40, 30, and 33 points, respectively. They then lost to Kansas—the eventual champion—by just two points. As a junior, Curry averaged 28.6 PPG and earned First Team All-American honors.

In 2009, Golden State selected Stephen with the seventh pick. Immediately, he reminded fans of Rick Barry, the legendary shooter who led the Warriors to their last NBA title in 1975. The rookie not only made a ton of three-pointers (166), but he also nailed them at a high rate (43.7 percent). In his second season, he led the NBA in free-throw percentage (93.4).

In 2012–13, Stephen took his shooting talents to new heights. He averaged 22.9 PPG, buried an NBA-record 272 threes, and shot them at a 45.3 percent clip. Curry released his shots in about 0.3 seconds, which made it difficult for defenders to get a hand in his face. The next season, he led in three-pointers again (261) and made his first NBA All-Star team. In 2014–15, he was so popular that he was the leading recipient of votes for the NBA All-Star Game, beating out LeBron James.

That season, Curry broke his own three-pointer record (286) and averaged 23.8 PPG. He and fellow long-range bomber Klay Thompson—the Splash Brother—led the Warriors to a 67–15 record and a spot in the NBA Finals. There, he faced LeBron James and the Cleveland Cavaliers. When asked how the Cavs would stop Curry, LeBron replied, "The same way you slow me down: You can't."

And they didn't. The Warriors defeated Cleveland in six games with Curry averaging 26.0 PPG. The player whom Virginia Tech didn't want was now an NBA champion.

★ Glossary ★

alma mater—The college or university that one attended.

boards—Another name for rebounds.

dehydrated—When a person's body has lost too much water.

fadeaway jumper—A jump shot taken while falling backward; such a shot is difficult for the defender to block.

fundamentals—The basic and essential aspects of sports, such as how to dribble and pass in basketball.

generation—A group of people born and living at the same time.

jump shot—A shot made while jumping and releasing the ball at the peak of the jump.

natural athlete—A person who easily excels at athletics.

post up—To play near the basket with one's back to the rim.

power forward—Typically a larger, stronger forward who plays close to the basket.

reverse layup—A layup in which a player starts at one side of the rim and then shoots the ball underhand at the other side of the rim.

scholarship—Money that a school gives to a student for his or her education.

set shot—A shot made while standing still.

small forward—Typically the smaller of the two forwards who are on the court; usually they are more athletic and a better shooter than the power forward.

triple-double—Double digits (10 or more) in three statistical categories—typically points, assists, and rebounds but could also include blocked shots and steals.

varsity—The top-level team at a high school, college, or university.

★ Further Reading ★

Books

Aaseng, Nathan. *Michael Jordan: Hall of Fame Basketball Superstar.* Berkeley Heights, NJ: Speeding Star, 2014.

Dayton, Connor. *Kobe Bryant: NBA Scoring Sensation.* New York: Britannica Educational/Rosen, 2016.

Graves, Will. *The Best NBA Guards of All Time.* Edina, MN: ABDO Publishing, 2015.

Kavanagh, Jack. *Larry Bird: Hall of Fame Basketball Superstar.* Berkeley Heights, NJ: Speeding Star, 2014.

Koepp, Stephen, ed. *Big Book of Who: Basketball.* New York: Sports Illustrated for Kids, 2015.

Norwich, Grace. *LeBron James.* New York: Scholastic Book Service, 2014.

Websites

Basketball Reference

basketball-reference.com

Includes statistics on every player in NBA history.

Jr. NBA

jr.nba.com

Sections include "Skills and Drills," "About the Game," "Fun Zone," and more.

National Basketball Association

nba.com

Loaded with everything NBA: player profiles, scores, stats, standings, news, and highlight videos, as well as Kids Club Fun and Games.

★ INDEX ★